HELLO, BUNNIES!

THE NEW NEIGHBORS

BY

Sarah McIntyre

FOR MY FABULOUS
NEIGHBORS
SUSI AND DAVID

PENGUIN WORKSHOP
Penguin Young Readers Group
An Imprint of Penguin Random House LLC

Copyright © 2018 by Sarah McIntyre. All rights reserved. First published in Great Britain in 2018 by David Fickling Books. Published in the United States in 2019 by Penguin Workshop, an imprint of Penguin Random House LLC, 345 Hudson Street, New York, New York 10014. PENGUIN and PENGUIN WORKSHOP are trademarks of Penguin Books Ltd, and the W colophon is a trademark of Penguin Random House LLC. Manufactured in China.

Library of Congress Cataloging-in-Publication Data is available.

ISBN 9781524789961   10 9 8 7 6 5 4 3 2 1

WITHDRAWN

Clovis   Oscar   Piper   Jake

ROSIE

High on the roof, above the city, Mr. Pigeon had the latest news.

"You've got RATS in your building!" he burbled with glee. "They moved in today on the first floor."

"RATS!" squealed the bunnies.
"RATS!
  RATS!
    RATS!
YIPPEE!!"

The bunnies were so
excited that they

BOUNCED

down

the

stairs

to tell their

big sister,

Lettuce.

"Guess what!" shouted Rosie.
"RATS have moved in!"

Lettuce said, "Hmm . . . RATS!
I've never lived with RATS before . . .

. . . We should go and say hi.

Let's see if Vern wants to come."

All the bunnies

HOPPED 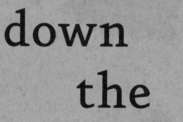 down
the
stairs.

"Hi, Vern!" said Lettuce.
"Some rats have just
moved in downstairs.
Do you want to come
and say hello?"

"RATS?" mused Vern. "I don't think rats are very tidy neighbors. We need to make sure they keep the place clean. Let's gather everyone in the building and figure out what to do."

The rabbits and Vern **HOPPED** and **TROTTED** downstairs to talk to the pigs.

WHOOSH

RRRR

"Walter! Matilda!" said Vern. "We have RATS in our building! We need to make sure these RATS know our rules about keeping this building spick-and-span."

"RATS?" grunted Walter. "Oh no!"

Matilda huffed. "Heavens! Rats are messy *and* they SMELL BAD, too. This is AWFUL news! I bet I know what the polar bears are going to say."

Everyone
HOPPED
and
TROTTED
and TOTTERED
downstairs . . .

"Lars! Astrid! You're not going to like this!" said Matilda. "Smelly, messy RATS just moved in downstairs!" "WHAT?" said Astrid. "Rats are smelly and messy . . . *and* they like to steal food!"

WHAT!?

BURP

EW!

Lars looked worried. "What will we eat if they steal all our food? We must tell the yaks this TERRIBLE NEWS!"

WOULD THEY STEAL MY TEDDY, TOO?

Everyone HOPPED and TROTTED and TOTTERED and PADDED downstairs . . .

"Norbu! Pemba! We're in trouble!" said Lars. "BIG TROUBLE! Dirty, stinking, thieving RATS are now living downstairs. And I've heard that rats love to chew through walls! The WHOLE BUILDING might fall down!"

Norbu and Pemba gasped in horror.

Pemba's voice trembled. "We must DO something!"

Everyone
HOPPED
and TROTTED
and TOTTERED
and PADDED
and CLATTERED
downstairs . . .

"OPEN THE DOOR, Granny Goat! This is an EMERGENCY!" shouted Norbu.

"RATS! BIG, DIRTY, SMELLY, THIEVING, DANGEROUS RATS have moved in downstairs and they are going to make the whole building collapse and bury us alive in RAT POOP!"

NO!! We must make them leave RIGHT NOW!

Granny Goat shrieked.

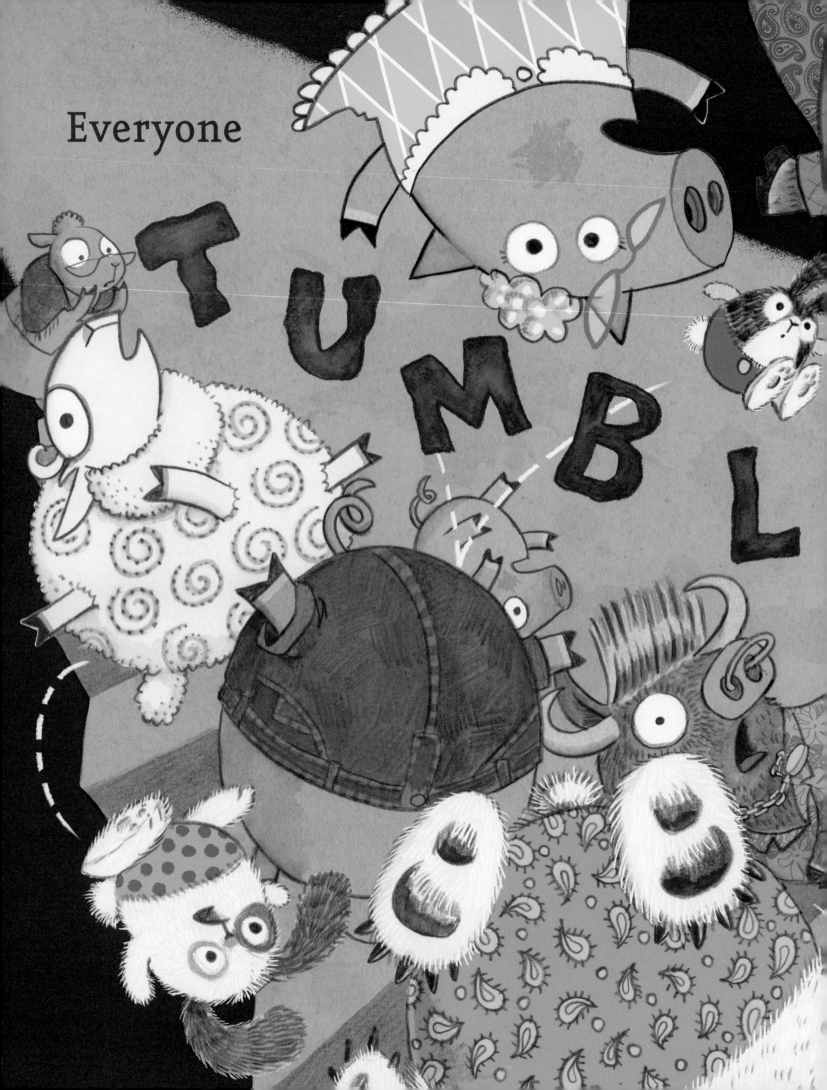

Everyone

downstairs and
fell at the bottom,
in a big pile.

They paused in front of the
rats' door. No one wanted
to be the first to knock.

. . . and a small,

tidy,

friendly-looking rat

smiled up at them.

"Hello! Are you our new
neighbors?" she asked.

Another small,

tidy rat

joined her.

"I'm Bertram and this is Natasha.
Will you join us for some
homemade cake?

We've just unpacked the dishes and were
planning to invite you over. Do come in!"

Everyone shuffled inside. They felt embarrassed—except the bunnies, who were excited about CAKE.

"How wonderful to have such thoughtful, welcoming new neighbors living here!" said Natasha.

"Yes," said Bertram. "We thought you might worry when you heard that rats had moved in. We know that rats aren't everyone's idea of the perfect neighbors!"

GULP

HEH
HEH...

"OH NO!" gasped
Lettuce through a
mouthful of carrot cake.
"That thought NEVER crossed our minds!"
All the animals nodded their heads and blushed.

After they gobbled up the last crumbs of cake, they HOPPED and TROTTED and TOTTERED and PADDED and CLATTERED back upstairs . . .

Jake burped.